Fishing at Long Pond

by William T. George

pictures by
Lindsay Barrett George

Greenwillow Books
New York

"Where are we going to fish today, Grampy?" Katie asked.
"I thought we'd row around the edge of the pond," said her grandfather.
"Where are the worms?" asked Katie.

"We're not going to use worms. Worms are good for sunfish and perch. Today you're going to catch your first bass—with this lure." Grandfather tapped his knuckles against the wooden boat. "Knock wood," he said. "All fishermen believe in luck." He smiled at Katie.

Grandfather rowed in a steady rhythm, leaving behind a trail
of double whirlpools. The oarlocks groaned and creaked.
He showed Katie how to trail the lure behind the boat.

"If a fish grabs it," he said, "lift up sharply
on the rod once, then let him go where he wants."

They passed some wildflowers.
"Can we pick some for Nanny?" Katie asked.

"You know Nanny likes wildflowers to stay right where they grow," said Grandfather. "Just remember to tell her you saw some wild irises."

Two deer came down to the pond's edge for an afternoon drink.
Grandfather stopped rowing, and the boat glided by noiselessly.

The deer snorted and bounded off through
the swamp azalea and blueberry bushes.

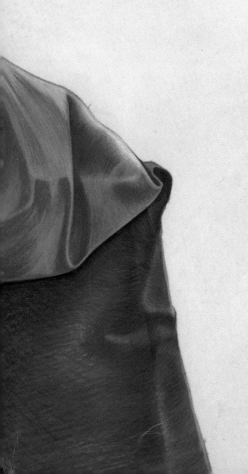

An osprey sailed over Long Pond.
He was searching for fish.
The bird stopped and hovered with
quick, backward wing beats.
Suddenly, he dropped from
the sky, his feet and sharp talons
outstretched below him.

SPLASH! The osprey plunged into the pond and
flew out, beating the water frantically with his wings.
A large, wriggling perch was locked in his claws.
"He's caught a fish!" Katie cried.
The osprey called loudly as he flew away—
SHRIEK! SHRIEK! SHRIEK!

The rowboat approached a small island. A large Canada goose plopped into the water and swam toward the boat. He honked loudly while bobbing his head.

"This goose is angry," Grandfather whispered. "His mate is on the island, sitting on her nest. It's the end of May, and her eggs should be hatching any day now. He does not want us to disturb her. Reel in your line, and we'll row by him."

The rowboat glided past an old beaver lodge.
The water swirled above the lure.
Grandfather smiled to himself.

"Get ready," he said slowly, in a quiet voice.
"You're about to get a strike."
The rod tip bounced down, and Katie yelled,
"I got him! I got him!"

Grandfather rowed the boat out to deeper water.
The taut line rose to the surface.
"He's going to jump," Grandfather said. "When he
jumps, don't pull back hard."

The bass leaped high into the air,
shaking his head.

The fish made three more jumps, each lower than the last.
Then Grandfather was able to lift the fish up into the boat.
"A two-pounder, for sure. Look at that," he said proudly.

"Why, he's barely hooked at all, just under the skin.
It was your light touch that caught him."
Grandfather slipped the fish into the well under
his seat and began to row.

Swallows soared and dove through the air, catching insects in their mouths. A beaver swam toward the outlet, dragging a green branch in his mouth.

"Let's reel in your line," Grandfather said, "and get ready to tie up at the dock. Nanny's waiting for us. We've got a fish to cook for dinner."

TO DAD, WHO ROWED THE BOAT
AND PROTECTS THE POND

Special thanks to Hope Carpenter
of the Pennsylvania Raptor and Wildlife Association

Gouache paints were used for the full-color art.
The text type is ITC Leawood.

Printed in Hong Kong by South China Printing Company (1988) Ltd.
First Edition   10 9 8 7 6 5 4 3 2 1

Library of Congress Cataloging-in-Publication Data

George, William T.
Fishing at Long Pond / by William T. George ;
pictures by Lindsay Barrett George.
p.   cm.
Summary: While fishing for bass, Katie and her grandfather
observe a deer, an osprey, a goose, and other pond visitors.
ISBN 0-688-09401-5.   ISBN 0-688-09402-3 (lib. bdg.)
[1. Fishing—Fiction.   2. Grandfathers—Fiction.
3. Animals—Fiction.]   I. George, Lindsay Barrett, ill.
II. Title. PZ7.G29344Fi   1991
[E]—dc20   89-77514   CIP   AC